W9-ATY-418

WITHDRAWN
**MANDEL PUBLIC LIBRARY
OF WEST PALM BEACH**
411 Clematis Street
West Palm Beach, FL 33401
(561) 868-7700

CALICO ILLUSTRATED CLASSICS

Louisa May Alcott's

Little Women

ADAPTED BY: Kathryn Lay
ILLUSTRATED BY: Mike Lacey

magic
Wagon

MANDEL PUBLIC LIBRARY OF W
411 CLEMATIS STREET
WEST PALM BEACH, FL 33401
(561) 868-7700

visit us at www.abdopublishing.com

Published by Magic Wagon, a division of the ABDO Group,
8000 West 78th Street, Edina, Minnesota 55439. Copyright
© 2012 by Abdo Consulting Group, Inc. International copyrights
reserved in all countries. All rights reserved. No part of this
book may be reproduced in any form without written permission
from the publisher.

Calico Chapter Books™ is a trademark and logo of Magic Wagon.

Printed in the United States of America, Melrose Park, Illinois.
042011
092011

 This book contains at least 10% recycled materials.

Original text by Louisa May Alcott
Adapted by Kathryn Lay
Illustrated by Mike Lacey
Edited by Stephanie Hedlund and Rochelle Baltzer
Cover and interior design by Abbey Fitzgerald

Library of Congress Cataloging-in-Publication Data

Lay, Kathryn.
  Louisa May Alcott's Little women / adapted by Kathryn Lay ;
illustrated by Mike Lacey.
      p. cm. -- (Calico illustrated classics)
  ISBN 978-1-61641-617-1
  [1. Family life--New England--Fiction. 2. Sisters--Fiction. 3. New
England--History--19th century--Fiction.] I. Lacey, Mike, ill. II.
Alcott, Louisa May, 1832-1888. Little women. III. Title.
  PZ7.L445Lp 2011
  [Fic]--dc22
                                        2011002735

Table of Contents

CHAPTER 1

Presents for Marmee

"It won't be Christmas without any presents," grumbled Jo.

Meg sighed, "It's awful being poor!"

Little Amy sniffed. "It's not fair that some girls have lots of nice things and others have nothing."

"We've got Father and Mother and each other," Beth said happily from her corner.

They each thought of Father far away in the fighting. Meg said, "Mother knows it will be a hard winter. She thinks we should not spend money on pleasures when the men suffer in the army."

"We each have a dollar and that won't help the army much. I would like to buy a new book," said Jo, who loved to read.

Beth said with a quiet sigh, "I plan to buy new music."

"I will buy a nice box of drawing pencils," Amy said.

"Mother didn't say we couldn't spend our own money. We work hard for it," said Jo.

They each agreed that they worked hard with Meg teaching, Jo taking care of fussy old Aunt March, Beth keeping the house tidy, and Amy going to school with girls who laughed at her for being poor.

Margaret was sixteen, very pretty, and a bit vain. Fifteen-year-old Jo was tall and thin. Beth was thirteen and shy. She seemed happy to live in a world of her own. Amy was pretty with blue eyes and yellow hair. She always carried herself like a young lady.

When the clock struck six, Beth put a pair of slippers by the fireplace to warm. The girls knew their mother was coming and they all cheered up. Jo held the slippers nearer to the fire.

"These are old and Marmee needs a new pair," Jo said.

Beth said, "Why don't each of us get Marmee something for Christmas and nothing for ourselves?"

Everyone agreed. They decided to surprise her. They would shop the next afternoon.

"I shall get her a nice pair of gloves," Meg said.

"The best shoes," cried Jo.

"Some handkerchiefs," said Beth.

"And a little bottle of cologne," added Amy.

While they waited, they spent time practicing their annual Christmas play. When they were done, Beth said, "I don't see how you can write such wonderful things, Jo."

As they laughed together, a cheery voice said, "Glad to find you so happy, my girls."

The girls welcomed their mother, who they thought was the most splendid mother in the world. As she asked about each of them, they hurried around her to make her comfortable.

Mrs. March said, "I have a treat for you after supper."

Beth clapped her hands and Jo tossed up her napkin shouting, "A letter from Father!"

They hurried through their dinner. Then, their mother read the letter. At the end, Father gave his love and a kiss to each. *"I think of them every day and pray for them at night. I know they will remember everything I said to them and they will be loving children to you, work hard, and be good girls so that when I come back I may be prouder than ever of my little women."*

They each cried and promised to not be so selfish. Then they sat and sewed without complaining at all. At nine they stopped and sang, as usual, before going to bed. Beth knew how to softly touch the yellow keys of the old piano and make it sound good. They never grew too old for their singing time every night.

A Merry Christmas

Jo woke up Christmas morning and was disappointed at first that there were no stockings full of goodies. Then she remembered her mother's promise. Under her pillow was a little red-covered book, *Pilgrim's Progress*.

Each girl woke up with the book with a different color cover under her pillow. When they ran downstairs to thank their mother, they found Hannah, who had lived there since Meg was born.

"Some poor person came begging and your ma went to help," Hannah said.

Everyone put their gifts for their mother into a basket. They heard the front door open and close. They hid the basket and hurried to the breakfast table.

"Merry Christmas, Marmee! Thank you for our books," they cried.

"Merry Christmas, daughters. I want to tell you about the poor woman nearby with a newborn baby. Six children crowd into one bed to stay warm. There is nothing to eat. Will you give them your breakfast as a Christmas gift?"

Everyone wanted to help carry the food to the children. They soon were in a bare and miserable room with broken windows and no fire. The sick mother and hungry children smiled at the girls.

"You are angels," the woman cried.

Quickly they made a fire, fixed the broken windows with old hats, and fed the family as if they were hungry birds.

When they returned home, they shouted, "Three cheers for Marmee!" and sat their mother in a seat of honor. She was surprised as they gave her their gifts. Then they presented their play.

Afterward, Hannah appeared and invited them to go to supper. When they saw the table, they were amazed. There was ice cream, cake, fruit, and French candies. In the middle of the table were four bouquets of flowers.

Mrs. March said, "Old Mr. Laurence sent it."

"The Laurence boy's grandfather from next door? We don't even know him," Meg said.

Their mother explained, "Hannah told one of his servants about what you did with your breakfast. He sent a note saying he wanted to send these to you in honor of the day."

Someday, they hoped to get to know the old man who lived next door.

The Laurence Boy

A few days later, Meg ran upstairs and waved a piece of paper at Jo. "It's an invitation from Mrs. Gardiner for you and me to go to a dance on New Year's Eve!" Meg shouted.

They talked and argued about clothes for the party. Meg worried that their dresses weren't nice enough.

The day of the party, Jo burned Meg's hair with the curling papers, but finally they were ready to go.

"Have a good time," Mrs. March called.

Mrs. Gardiner greeted them kindly. Meg felt comfortable with Mrs. Gardiner's daughter, but Jo stood with her back against the wall, feeling out of place. She slipped behind some curtains to watch the party. But another shy person had chosen the same place to hide. She found herself face-to-face with the "Laurence boy."

"Oh dear," Jo stammered.

The boy laughed. He admitted that he hid because he didn't know many people. Jo said it was the same reason she hid. She thanked him for the Christmas surprise from his grandfather.

"My name is Jo," she said.

"I'm Laurie," he said.

Laurie told Jo about his time in school far away and how they went on walking trips around Switzerland with their teachers.

"Oh," said Jo, "did you go to Paris?"

"Last winter," Laurie said.

In French he asked, "Who is the young lady in the pretty slippers?"

Jo said, "It's my sister Margaret. Do you think she is pretty?"

"Yes," Laurie said. "She dances like a lady."

Jo and Laurie watched the party and talked until they felt like old friends. She liked him

and remembered how he looked so she could tell her sisters.

Curly black hair, brown skin, big black eyes, handsome nose, fine teeth, taller than I am, polite for a boy, and happy. I wonder how old he is? Jo thought.

She asked and he said that he would be sixteen the next month.

Meg came in then and motioned to Jo to follow her. Jo found her sitting on a sofa, holding her foot.

"I've sprained my ankle. I can hardly stand," Meg said.

"I knew you'd hurt your feet in those silly shoes," Jo said. "I'm sorry, but you'll have to get a carriage ride home."

Meg shook her head. "It will cost too much. Go to dinner but don't say anything about me."

After dinner, Laurie appeared with a plate of ice and a cup of coffee.

"May I take this to your sister?" he asked.

Jo took him to where Meg waited and they all had a nice time eating chocolates and playing a quiet game until it was time to go home. Laurie offered his grandfather's carriage. It began to rain as they rolled away.

"I had a wonderful time," Jo told Meg.

"I did too until I hurt myself. Annie Moffat invited me to spend a week with her and even go to the opera," Meg said. She told Jo about the man she danced with and got angry at Jo when she said her and Laurie had been laughing at the man's dancing.

When they returned home Amy and Beth begged to hear about the party. Jo gave them candy she had saved for them.

"I feel like a fine lady coming home in a carriage," Meg said.

Jo added, "I don't believe fine young ladies enjoy themselves more than we do, in spite of our burned hair, old gowns, one glove apiece, and tight slippers that sprain our ankles."

CHAPTER
4

Being Neighborly

Since the party, Jo had wanted to get to know the "Laurence boy." As she swept the snow one day, she saw the top of his head in a window. She tossed a handful of snow at it.

"Are you sick?" she called out.

Laurie opened the window a little. "I've had a bad cold and been shut up a week. Will you come and visit, please?"

Jo promised to come if her mother let her.

Laurie was full of excitement as he ran around and tidied his room. Soon he heard a servant announcing a young lady at the door. Jo walked into the room with a dish of sweet dessert and Beth's three kittens.

Laurie laughed at the kittens. He asked about Jo's sisters. "When I'm alone up here, sometimes, I look at your house and you seem to be having such good times. I haven't got a mother, you know."

Jo felt sorry for him. "You can come over and see us. Mother is wonderful and Beth will sing to you. Amy would dance. Meg and I would make you laugh."

They talked about books and Jo told him stories of her Aunt March that made him laugh. Laurie left her for a moment and Jo stared at Mr. Laurence's portrait.

"He seems grim, but he's got kind eyes," Jo said to the room. "I shouldn't be afraid. He isn't as handsome as my grandfather, but I like him."

"Thank you," a rough voice said.

Jo saw to her horror that old Mr. Laurence had entered the room. She blushed and saw that his eyes were even kinder than in the portrait. But his gruff voice said, "So you're not afraid of me?"

"Not much, sir," said Jo.

"And you like me?"

"Yes, I do, sir," she said.

He laughed. "If you'd like to come downstairs to tea, you're welcome," he said.

Jo agreed and wondered what Meg would say about this! She and Laurie followed him into a great drawing room. He stood by a grand piano.

"Do you play?" Jo asked Laurie.

"Sometimes," he said.

"Please let me hear so I can tell Beth."

He played very well and Jo wished Beth could hear him. When she praised him, his grandfather stood up quickly, shook her hand, and left.

"Did I say something wrong?" she asked.

Laurie said, "He doesn't like to hear me play."

As she left, she promised to come again. After she told everyone at home of her adventures, they all wanted to go visit.

"Why doesn't he like Laurie to play the piano, Mother?" Jo asked.

"I think it was because Laurie's father ran away and married an Italian lady who was a musician. They died when Laurie was young and his grandfather brought him home. He is also afraid Laurie will want to be a musician like his mother."

When Jo asked her mother if Laurie could come see them, she agreed that he could. The new friendship between the Marches and the Laurences soon grew.

After they got used to Mr. Laurence, they had wonderful times together doing plays, going on sleigh rides, and even having a few parties at the great house.

Meg walked through the indoor garden whenever she wanted, while Jo enjoyed the new library. Amy copied pictures, and Laurie played "lord of the manor."

Beth longed to see the piano. She went once with Jo, but old Mr. Laurence frightened her with his loud voice. So, she ran away and promised never to go back.

During one of Mr. Laurence's visits to the March house, he told stories about music and soon Beth crept nearer. He talked about how Laurie did not work on his music. "I'm glad of it, but the piano suffers from not being used. Wouldn't some of your girls like to come and practice on it?" he asked.

Beth moved a step forward.

"They wouldn't even have to talk to anyone, just come and play," he continued. "I am usually in my study on the other side of the house."

Then Beth slipped her hand into his and told him how much she loved music. She blushed and gave his hand a thankful squeeze.

The next day, after she saw the Laurences leave their house, she snuck into the house and to the room where the beautiful piano stood. With fingers that trembled, Beth finally touched the great piano and soon forgot her fear.

She stayed until Hannah came to take her home for dinner. Beth smiled at everyone instead of eating. After that, she went nearly every day. She never knew that Mr. Laurence often opened his study door to listen.

"Mother," Beth said a few weeks later, "I'm going to make Mr. Laurence a pair of slippers. He is so kind to me."

Beth worked hard on the slippers. With Laurie's help they snuck them onto Mr. Laurence's table one morning. It was almost two days before anything happened. Then a letter came for Beth.

"Look, he's sent you . . ." Amy began, but Jo stopped her until Beth came into the house.

In the parlor sat a little piano.

"For me?" Beth gasped, holding on to Jo.

They begged her to read the letter, but she said, "Read it, Jo, I'm too excited."

Jo read, "I've never had slippers that I liked better. I know you will allow 'the old gentleman' to send you something that once belonged to the granddaughter he lost. Your grateful friend, James Laurence."

Beth tried the pretty piano. Everyone said it was the most wonderful piano they ever heard.

"You should go thank him," Jo said, knowing Beth would not do such a thing.

But Beth amazed them all by standing up and saying, "Yes, I will do it now."

They would have been even more amazed if they had seen her go to the study, throw her arms around him, and kiss him.

He walked her home, shook her hand, and touched his hat as he left. When the girls saw, Jo began to dance, Amy nearly fell out of the window in surprise, and Meg said, "I do believe the world is coming to an end!"

Jo Learns to Forgive

Amy came into the room one Saturday afternoon to find Jo and Meg getting ready to go somewhere.

"Where are you going?" she asked.

"Little girls shouldn't ask questions," Jo said.

Amy saw Meg put a fan into her pocket. "You're going with Laurie to the theater! I want to go. I want to go with you and Laurie. I'll be good," she begged.

Meg turned to Jo. "Maybe we could take her."

"If she goes, I won't!" Jo shouted. "Laurie already has our seats and if she goes he'll have to be nice and let her have his. It will ruin the evening."

When Laurie called from downstairs, Amy screamed, "You'll be sorry for this, Jo March!"

Jo slammed the door as they left. When they got home, Amy was sitting in the parlor reading. She never looked up at them. Jo ran to her dresser in her room. The last time she and Amy had fought, Amy had emptied out Jo's top drawer. But this time, everything was in its place.

The next day Jo discovered something was missing. She ran into the parlor and asked, "Has anyone taken my book?"

Meg and Beth were quick to say no. Amy poked the fire and was quiet.

"You've got it!" Jo yelled at Amy.

Amy shouted, "You'll never see your silly old book again! I burned it."

Jo turned pale. She had worked so hard on the little book, filling with her own writing. They were stories Jo had worked on for years. She wanted to have it all filled before Father returned. Now it was burned!

At teatime, Amy gathered her courage and said, "Please forgive me, Jo."

"Never!" Jo answered. She ignored Amy from then on.

When Mrs. March kissed Jo good night she whispered, "Don't let the sun go down on your anger. Forgive each other."

But Jo said, "She doesn't deserve to be forgiven."

The next morning, Jo decided to ask Laurie to go skating. When Amy heard the noise of the skates, she cried, "Jo promised I could go with them next time. Today is the last time the ice will be good."

"Go after them," Meg said. "Be kind and Jo will be friends again."

But when Jo saw Amy following behind, she turned away. Laurie did not see her. Jo skated down the river, ignoring Amy. Laurie shouted, "It's not safe in the middle, stay near the shore!"

But Amy did not hear him. She skated toward the smooth ice in the middle. Jo began to skate farther away, but turned in time to see Amy fall through the ice.

Jo couldn't scream or move. Laurie rushed past her, "Quick, bring a fence rail!"

Jo dragged a rail from the fence as Laurie held Amy up by his arm. Together they pulled her out. She was more frightened than hurt.

Laurie wrapped his coat around Amy and they hurried her home. She finally fell asleep, rolled in blankets near a hot fire.

"Is she safe?" Jo whispered to her mother.

"Yes, thanks to you and Laurie for covering her and getting her home quick."

Jo fell down beside the bed and cried. "It will be my fault if she dies. It's all because of my awful temper."

Amy moved in her sleep. Jo looked up and said, "I did let the sun go down on my anger. If it hadn't been for Laurie today, I might never have been able to tell her I forgive her."

Amy opened her eyes and held out her arms. Neither she nor Jo said a word, but they hugged one another and everything was forgiven and forgotten.

CHAPTER
6

Secrets

In the evenings, Jo worked quietly in the attic. She wrote and wrote until the last page was filled, then signed her name and threw down her pen.

"I've done my best!" she announced.

She read her story, making changes here and there. Then she took another story she'd written from an old tin box. She crept downstairs as quiet as she could, put on her hat and jacket, and snuck out a back window.

Jo took a cab to town, being very mysterious for anyone who might be watching. She went inside a doorway, but ran out three times before going inside the building.

A young gentleman watched and waited outside. Jo saw him as she came out ten minutes later. She hurried past, but he followed her and said, "You are up to some kind of mischief."

Jo tried to ignore Laurie.

"If you are nice, I'll walk with you and tell you something interesting," Laurie said. "It's a secret. Then you must tell me yours."

Jo started to say she had none, but remembered that she did. After making him promise not to tease, she whispered, "I have left two stories with a newspaperman. He will tell me next week if he'll publish them."

"Hurrah!" Laurie shouted, throwing his hat in the air.

"Hush," Jo said. "Nothing will come of it, but I had to try. I haven't told anyone else so they won't be disappointed."

But Laurie praised her stories and made her eyes sparkle. She asked, "What is your secret?"

He said, "I know where Meg's lost glove is."

Jo looked disappointed. Meg had lost her glove at the New Year's party ages ago. The March girls had long forgotten about it.

"Is that all?" she asked.

Laurie said, "And here is where it is." He leaned forward to whisper in Jo's ear.

Jo looked upset. "How do you know?"

"Saw it," he said. "In a pocket. Isn't that romantic?"

"No," Jo said. "It's horrible. What would Meg say?"

Laurie asked her not to tell anyone. "I thought you'd be happy."

Jo cried, "I'm disgusted. I wish you hadn't told me."

For a week, Jo behaved strangely. Her sisters were worried. She ran to the door when the postman came, was rude to Mr. Brooke, and looked at Meg sadly.

On the second Saturday, Jo and Laurie ran outside laughing, then came back in with the papers. Jo pretended to read.

"Anything interesting?" Meg asked.

"Oh, just a story." Jo kept the name of the paper hidden.

"Read it out loud," Amy said.

Jo took a long breath and read the story very fast. The girls listened with interest. They all agreed how much they liked it.

"Who wrote it?" asked Beth.

Jo jumped up and shouted, "Your sister."

"You?" Meg cried, dropping her sewing.

"It's very good," Amy said.

Beth ran to hug her and shouted, "I knew it! I'm so proud!"

They all stood around Jo, laughing and talking at once. Jo told them all about taking the story to the newspaperman. "He said he liked them both, but he doesn't pay beginners. I shall write more and he's going to get the next paid for. I am so happy!"

Jo ran out of breath, wrapped her head in the paper, and cried onto the story. To take care of herself and hear the praise of those she loved were the dearest wishes of her heart. She was on the first step to such a happy ending.

Dark Days

One day, Hannah answered the door and returned to Mrs. March with a telegram. It read: *Mrs. March, your husband is very ill. Come at once.*

Mrs. March rushed around shouting at everyone to get her trunk, nursing supplies, and anything else her husband might need or want.

Mr. Laurence came with more things to help Mr. March. As Meg ran through the hall, she ran suddenly into Mr. Brooke.

"I'm sorry to hear about this," he said. "I will go with your mother since Mr. Laurence has things for me to do in Washington."

"How kind of you!" Mcg said. "Thank you!"

Soon, everything was ready. Then Jo gave her mother a roll of money.

"Twenty-five dollars! Jo, what have you done?" her mother asked.

"I earned it and I sold what was my own," Jo said. She took off her hat and everyone cried out. Her long hair was cut short.

Jo said, "It doesn't affect the fate of the country, so don't be upset. I wanted to do something for Father. I had to find some way to get some money."

As they waited for the carriage the next morning, their mother said, "Children, I leave you to Hannah's care and Mr. Laurence's protection. Don't worry while I am gone. Do your work as usual."

They each promised to do the things she asked. The carriage drove away and the sun shone on their smiling faces as they waved.

Over the next few weeks, news from their father gave them comfort. He was dangerously ill, but the care of his nurses had already helped him. Mr. Brooke sent a note every day, and the news was always better.

For the next week, everyone worked hard. But after awhile they grew tired and stopped. In this, they learned a hard lesson.

"Meg, you should go see the Hummels. Mom told us not to forget them," Beth said. It had been ten days since their mother left.

"I'm too tired," Meg said. "Why don't you go?"

Beth said, "I have been every day, but the baby is sick. My head aches and I'm so tired."

Meg promised to go the next day. Jo said, "I'd go, but I want to finish my writing."

They waited to see if Amy would come home and go. But after an hour, she did not come. Meg went to her room to try on a new dress, Jo worked on her story, and Hannah was asleep by the fire. Beth quietly put on her coat, filled her basket with things for the poor children, and went into the cold air. It was late when she came home.

Not long later, Jo found her sitting in their mother's closet, looking sad and with red eyes.

"What's the matter?" Jo cried.

"Oh, Jo!" Beth said. "The baby died in my lap before Mrs. Hummel came home. The doctor came with her and said it is scarlet fever. He told me to go home and take medicine."

Jo hugged her and said, "If you get sick, I'll never forgive myself!"

Beth said she had the symptoms already.

Jo hurried to get Hannah, who said she would get the doctor and send Amy to Aunt March's for a while. Jo promised to stay home and take care of Beth since she'd already had the fever before.

Amy threw a fit saying she would not go to Aunt March. But when Laurie came, he promised, "Don't cry. If you go, I'll come and take you out walking every day."

Amy slowly agreed to go. Laurie hurried off to get the doctor, who said that Beth might have it lightly. Jo and Laurie took Amy to Aunt March's right away.

As usual, Aunt March was harsh when Jo explained what happened.

"It's what I would expect if you go poking around poor people," Aunt March said. "Amy can stay and help me if she isn't sick."

Amy sniffed and said, "I don't think I can bear it here, but I'll try."

It turned out that Beth was very sick. Hannah told them not to worry their mother. Jo took care of Beth day and night. Beth never complained.

There was a time when Beth did not even know the faces around her, calling them by wrong names and asking for her mother. This frightened Jo and Meg. They begged to write the truth to their mother. Then a letter came from Washington saying their father was very ill again and it would be a long time before Marmee would be coming home.

The days seemed dark, sad, and lonely. The sisters worked and waited as death seemed to shadow the house.

Everyone who visited asked how Beth was and sent good wishes. She sent loving messages to Amy and told everyone to tell her mother she would write soon. But soon she was rarely awake, sleeping hour after hour.

On the first of December, Dr. Bangs came to check over Beth. He whispered to Hannah, "If Mrs. March can leave her husband, she better come home now."

Hannah nodded quietly, Meg fell into a chair, and Jo ran to send the telegram. Laurie came with a letter saying that Mr. March was well again, but when he saw Jo's face he asked, "Is Beth worse?"

Jo said, "I've sent for Mother. The doctor told us to."

Laurie cried, "It's not as bad as that is it?"

Jo explained that it was and that Beth didn't know anyone. "Mother and Father are both gone and there's no one to help us bear this."

Tears streamed down her face and Laurie took her hand. "I'm here, Jo dear!"

After crying for a while she said, "Thank you, Teddy," using her nickname for him.

Laurie told her a surprise. "I sent a message to your mother yesterday and asked her to come. She'll be here tonight."

Jo stared at him, then threw her arms around his neck. "I am so glad!"

Laurie said, "Grandpa and I thought your mother ought to know. I will go meet her at the train. Keep Beth quiet until she gets here."

Everyone rejoiced but Beth, who lay in a heavy sleep. It was a sad sight to see her face changed, her once busy hands so weak, and her beautiful hair tangled on the pillow.

It was after two in the morning when Jo heard a noise and turned to see Meg kneeling by their mother's chair. Jo thought, *Beth is dead and Meg is afraid to tell me.*

She hurried back to Beth and saw there was a change. The feverish look and pain was gone. Hannah jumped up, felt Beth's hands, listened at her lips, then sat down. She covered her head with her apron. "The fever has changed. She's sleepin' natural. Oh my goodness!"

The doctor came and agreed, "I think she will get well now."

"If only Mother would come!" Jo said.

As the sun rose, Meg said, "It looks like a fairy world."

Then there was a sound of bells at the door. Laurie said, "Girls, she's come!"

A Secret Told

The house was full of happiness at the reunion of the mother and her daughters. When Beth woke, the first thing she saw was her mother's face. Marmee sat and held Beth's thin hand as she slept.

After a large breakfast from Hannah, stillness and rest filled the house. Laurie hurried to tell Amy the news. Even Aunt March sniffed back tears at his story.

Later at home, Jo found Marmee in Beth's room and asked to speak to her quietly. "It's about Meg."

"Do you think he cares for her?" Mother asked.

"I don't know about love and such silliness," Jo said.

Her mother said, "Mr. Brooke asked me to call him by his first name. He's been so good to your father."

Jo was upset, but her mother said, "I will not agree to Meg getting engaged so young."

Jo argued, "He'll make her fall in love with him and he'll find a fortune somehow and take her away from our family. Let's send him away and not tell Meg."

Her mother said, "This is the way of girls. Meg's only seventeen and it will be years before John can make a home for her. If they love one another, they can wait."

A moment later, Meg came upstairs with a letter for her father.

"Add my love to John," Mrs. March said.

Meg smiled. "You call him John?"

Her mother nodded. "He has been like a son to us."

Meg said, "I'm glad. He is so lonely. Good night, Mother. I'm so glad to have you home."

Once, Jo found a piece of paper in Meg's desk with the words, "Mrs. John Brooke." Jo groaned and threw it in the fire.

The next weeks were filled with peace as the sick quickly improved. Mr. March talked of returning home early in the New Year. The girls took care of Beth in their own ways.

As Christmas came near, Jo and Laurie came up with all kinds of exciting ideas. But, they were soon stopped from their plans.

On Christmas Day, the weather was mild and Hannah "felt in her bones" it would be a wonderful day. Mr. March wrote that he would soon be home.

Beth felt much better and was carried to the window. Laurie and Jo had turned the garden into a surprise. A tall snow maiden stood, holding a basket of fruit and flowers in one hand and a roll of new music in the other. A colorful afghan hung around her shoulders and a paper streamer came out of her mouth with a Christmas carol for Beth.

Jo and Laurie ran outside to bring in the gifts to everyone. Then Laurie opened the parlor door and quietly said, "Here's another Christmas gift for the March family."

There stood a tall man leaning on the arm of another tall man. Everyone ran and soon Mr. March was surrounded by four pairs of loving arms.

Mrs. March finally held up her hand and said, "Hush! Remember Beth!"

But Beth ran into the room and straight into her father's arms. The two sick people were led to a big chair that they shared. Mr. March explained he had long wanted to surprise them.

When Mr. March glanced at Meg and suggested that Mr. Brooke eat something with them, Jo stormed out of the room.

Hannah had a Christmas dinner ready that was a sight to see. Mr. Laurence and Laurie ate with them. They all ate and drank and told stories and sang songs. Then, the guests left early so the family could be alone together.

Jo reminded them that a year before they were complaining about the small Christmas they would have. Mr. March spoke to each girl of how proud he was of them and the wonderful changes he could see in each.

When asked her thoughts, Beth told how in *Pilgrim's Progress* there were so many troubles and then a pleasant green meadow. "It's singing time now and I want to be in my old place."

Beth sat at the piano and softly touched the keys. She sang in a sweet voice that they had never thought to hear again.

The next day, mother, daughters, and even Hannah did everything to take care of Mr. March. But something seemed needed to complete their happiness.

Jo shook her fist at Mr. Brooke's umbrella left in the hall. Meg was shy and silent and blushed whenever John's name was said.

Jo said, "You are not your old self and seem so far away from me. I do wish it was all settled with you and Mr. Brooke. What would you say if he asked to marry you?"

Meg said, "I would calmly tell him that he is very kind but I agree with Father. I am too young and we should just be friends as before."

Then a knock at the door caused Meg to run to her seat and sew as fast as she could.

"Good afternoon, I came for my umbrella— and to see how your father is today," said Mr. Brooke as he walked into the room.

Jo said she would get their father and left to give Meg time to make her speech. But when Jo left the room, Meg moved toward the door. "Mother would like to see you, I'm sure."

"Don't go. Are you afraid of me, Margaret?" Mr. Brooke said, looking hurt.

Meg blushed and said, "You have been so kind to Father. I wish I could thank you."

Mr. Brooke held her small hand in his. "Shall I tell you how?" His eyes looked at her with so much love, her heart beat fast.

She tried to pull her hand away. He said, "Please, I love you so much. Do you care for me, Meg?"

She stammered that she didn't know and was too young. Finally she pulled her hand and said, "No, please leave."

John spoke so kindly and looked so sad that she found her heart changing. Just as John was leaving, Aunt March came in to see their father, her nephew.

"What's all this?" Aunt March asked.

"It's Father's friend," Meg said.

"I insist on knowing what's going on," Aunt March said, sitting down.

"Mr. Brooke just came for his umbrella," Meg said.

"That Laurence boy's tutor? I understand. I made Jo tell me about it. But, you haven't accepted him have you?" cried Aunt March.

Meg begged her to be quiet, but Aunt March said, "If you plan on marrying him, I'll leave you none of my money."

Meg said, "I shall marry who I please and you can give your money to whoever you want."

Aunt March stared at her. "Meg, I mean my advice kindly. You should marry someone rich and help your family."

"Mother and Father like John," Meg said.

They argued over whether Mr. Brooke had enough money or had any kind of business.

"I couldn't do better if I waited half my life," Meg said. "John is good and wise and has lots of talent and is willing to work hard. He cares for me even though I'm poor and young and silly."

"He knows you have rich relatives," Aunt March said.

Meg cried, "How dare you say such a thing! I won't listen to you. We are willing to work and to wait. I'm not afraid of being poor and I know I will be with him because he loves me and I—"

Aunt March was very angry. "You are a willful child. Don't expect anything from me when you are married. I'm done with you forever."

Then Mr. Brooke came and said, "I couldn't help hearing. Thank you for defending me. You prove you care for me a little."

"I didn't know until she was so mean to you," began Meg. She hid her face in John's coat and said, "You can stay."

Jo came and listened at the door. Hearing nothing, she thought that Meg had sent Mr.

Brooke away as promised. She went in and stared in shock at her sister sitting on Mr. Brooke's knee, looking at him with love.

Mr. Brooke laughed and said, "Sister Jo, congratulate us!"

Jo ran upstairs and shouted, "Somebody come quick!"

Mr. and Mrs. March ran out of the room while Jo cried and told Beth and Amy the awful news.

There was a good deal of talking that afternoon in the parlor. Mr. Brooke talked of what he would do to work while they waited for the wedding. Laurie danced into the room with flowers for "Mrs. John Brooke."

"I knew John would have his own way," Laurie said.

Jo did not approve of the match but made up her mind to not say anything against it. "I've lost my dearest friend," she told Laurie.

Laurie told her that she still had him and he would stand by her all his life.

The First Wedding

The three years that passed brought few changes to the quiet family. The war ended and Mr. March was safely at home, now a minister. Mrs. March spent a great deal of time getting ready for Meg's wedding.

John Brooke went to war for a year, got wounded, and was sent home. He worked hard to get well and earn money for a home for Meg.

Meg grew strong in character and learned how to take care of a home. She felt herself the luckiest girl around.

Jo never went back to work for Aunt March, who took quite a liking to Amy. She bribed Amy with drawing lessons. Jo devoted herself to books and Beth, who stayed delicate long after her illness.

The newspaper paid Jo a dollar a column. Jo was happy, yet still hoped for something more. She worked on a larger manuscript that grew bigger in the little tin box.

Laurie went to college to please his grandfather. He was a favorite at school because of his money, manners, talent, and kind heart. He would have become spoiled except for those who loved him back home.

Meg and her mother worked hard to prepare the home that Meg would have with John. She learned from Hannah how things should be done.

Finally, it came time for John to get the marriage license for the wedding.

Jo went for a walk with Laurie. They talked about his grandfather and how much money Laurie spent while at college. He talked about a boy named Parker, who was in love with Amy.

Jo said, "We don't want any more marrying in this family for years to come."

"You'll go next Jo," Laurie said.

"No one will want me," Jo said. "There should always be one old maid in a family."

Laurie said, "I promise, you will be next."

On the day of Meg's wedding, June roses bloomed over the porch. Meg looked like a rose as well. She would not wear silk, lace, or orange flowers.

"I don't want to look strange or fixed up," she said. "I just want those around me who I love and I want to look like my old self."

She made her own wedding gown and her sisters braided her pretty hair with lilies of the valley, which John liked. The three sisters wore suits of thin silver gray and had small roses in their hair. Everything was to be as natural and homelike as possible. When Aunt March arrived, she was shocked to see the bride run to greet her and find the bridegroom putting up flowers that had fallen.

"You shouldn't be seen till the last minute," Aunt March said.

But Meg declared she wasn't a show. "I'm going to have my wedding just as I like it," she said, giving John a hammer.

A crash and a laugh from Laurie came as he shouted, "Jo's upset the cake again!"

There was no bridal procession, but silence came over the group as Mr. March and the young couple took their places under the green arch of flowers.

Jo did not cry as Meg looked straight into her husband's eyes and said, "I will."

Beth kept her face hidden on her mother's shoulder and Amy stood like a graceful statue.

The minute she was married, Meg shouted, "The first kiss for Marmee!" and gave her mother a heartfelt kiss.

After lunch, people walked in groups of two and three through the house and garden.

Laurie shouted, "All the married people hold hands and dance around the new husband and wife! The unmarried men and women dance in couples outside the circle."

He grabbed Amy and danced until everyone followed them. Then Mr. Laurence walked up to Aunt March. She tucked her cane under her arm and hopped away to join hands with the others to dance around the bridal pair.

When Meg and her new husband led Aunt March to her carriage later, she told him, "You've got a treasure. See that you deserve it."

The couple's little house was close by. Meg came down the stairs looking pretty in a simple suit and hat. Everyone gathered around to tell her good-bye.

Meg said, "I'm not separated from you, Marmee, or will love you any less for loving John so much." She hugged her mother and promised her father to come every day. "Thank you all for a happy wedding day!"

They watched her go with faces full of love, hope, and pride. She leaned on her husband's arm. Her hands were full of flowers and the June sunshine brightened her happy face as Meg's married life began.

CHAPTER
10

Literary Lessons

Every few weeks, Jo would shut herself in her room and write away at her novel with all her heart and soul. One day in the street she noticed a boy reading a newspaper. He told her she could read it if she wanted. When she finished reading a story of love, mystery, and murder, the boy talked of how good a story it was and how much he liked it.

"The writer makes a good living out of these stories," the lad said.

Jo asked if he knew her. The boy explained that he did not, but read all her stories and knew a man who works in the newspaper office.

Jo could think of nothing but the address of the newspaper and decided to try for the $100 prize given for an amazing story.

Jo told no one her plans and went to work the next day. She'd never written such a dramatic story before. She sent the story to the newspaper and explained if it didn't win the prize, she would be very happy to get any amount of money they might decide it was worth.

Jo waited six weeks, keeping her secret from everyone. Then one day she opened a letter and a check for $100 fell into her lap. She read the letter and cried. The letter was encouraging and meant more to her than the money.

She proudly went to her family and showed them the letter and explained that she had won the prize. When the story came, everyone praised it.

Her father said, "Always aim for the best!"

Jo decided to use the money to send Beth and her mother to the beach for a month or two. Beth argued it was too much, but Jo talked her into going. And although Beth didn't come back as rosy as they had hoped, she was much better.

Jo earned more checks for her writing that year. She paid the bill to the butcher, put down a new carpet, and bought groceries and new gowns.

She decided to try for something even bigger. She copied her novel for the fourth time and then sent it in to three publishers. She was told that if she cut it down in size and cut out all the parts she liked most, it would be published.

"Don't spoil your book," her father said. "Wait and see."

Jo feared that she had worked on it so long, she didn't know any longer if it was good or bad. But Meg said the story would be spoiled if she left part of it out.

Amy thought she should do what the publisher, Mr. Allen, said. "He knows what will sell."

Jo asked Beth for her opinion. Beth said, "I would like to see it printed soon." The way she said the last word brought a chill to Jo's heart.

Jo took the book and cut parts of it, trying to please everyone, but instead pleasing no one. It was printed and she got $300 and lots of praise and blame.

Jo was confused and cried to her mother. "How can the critic's words help me if they say so many different things? I wish I'd printed it the way it was or not at all."

Her family and friends comforted her, but it was a hard time for Jo. Yet, after the first pain of it was over, she learned from what people said about her book and felt herself wiser and stronger.

She said, "The joke is on my side. The parts that were from real life were said impossible and the scenes I made up in my silly head are said to be natural and true. When I'm ready, I'll do another book."

Meg's New Life

Meg began her married life determined to be a model housekeeper. She wanted John to always find a happy home with a smiling wife and wonderful food. But she became too tired to even smile at times.

They were very happy. At first they played house and worked on it like children. Then John spent more time at business and Meg took to doing the work around the home.

A year went by and at midsummer, Meg became a mother.

Laurie snuck into the kitchen one Saturday. "How's the little momma? Why didn't you tell me?" Laurie said.

"She's happy as a queen," Hannah said. "They are all upstairs. I'll send them to you in the parlor."

Jo came, carrying a blanketed bundle. "Shut your eyes and hold out your arms."

"No, I'd rather not," Laurie said, backing into a corner. "I will drop it."

"Then you won't see it at all." Jo turned as if to go.

"Wait. But I won't be responsible." Laurie shut his eyes while something was put into his

arms. Laughter from Jo, Amy, Mrs. March, and Hannah caused him to open his eyes. He saw two babies instead of one.

"Twins!" he said. Then, he turned to the women and shouted, "Take them, quick! I'm going to laugh and I will drop them."

John rescued his babies and walked with one under each arm.

Laurie laughed and Jo said, "I wouldn't let anyone tell you, because I wanted to surprise you."

"It's a boy and girl. Aren't they beauties?" the proud father said. "The boy is named John Laurence and the girl Margaret. We shall call her Daisy so we won't have two Megs."

"Name the boy Demijohn and call him 'Demi'," Laurie said.

Jo clapped her hands. "I knew Teddy would pick it right. Daisy and Demi!"

CHAPTER 12

Amy Goes Abroad

One day a letter came from Aunt Carrol that made Mrs. March smile. "Aunt Carrol is going abroad next month and wants Amy to go with her."

Jo frowned. "Amy's too young. It's my turn first."

Mrs. March said that it was Amy who Aunt Carrol had invited.

"Amy has all the fun and I have all the work," cried Jo.

The letter explained that she had thought of inviting Jo, but Jo's blunt manners and hatred of French made her decide to ask Amy instead.

Amy went through her paints and drawing pencils. "This will decide my career," she said. "I shall find it in Rome and prove it."

Jo sewed new collars for Amy's clothes, her eyes red as she said, "What if you don't find it there?"

"Then I'll come home and teach drawing for my living," Amy said.

Jo said, "No, you won't. You don't like hard work and will marry some rich man. Your wishes are always granted—never mine."

Amy asked if Jo would like to go on the trip. She said yes. Amy said, "In a year or two I'll send for you."

There wasn't much time to get ready. Jo waited until Amy left and went off alone to cry until she couldn't cry any more. As the ship was about to leave, Amy realized that a whole ocean would soon be between her and those she loved. She hung on to Laurie and said, "Take care of them for me."

Amy sailed away to find the Old World, and her father and friend watched as she waved good-bye.

Amy wrote letters home about her adventures in London at Hyde Park and going to the theater. Old friends from home, Fred and Frank Vaughn, were in London and went along with them. She told of her many good times talking with them, especially Fred.

She told of a sailing trip up the Rhine River. At one time, Fred and students that he knew serenaded them all. Amy decided it was the most romantic thing she'd ever seen and they threw down flowers when the boys were done. She wrote:

The next morning, Fred showed me one of the crumpled flowers in his pocket. I told him it was not mine, but Flo's. He threw it out the window. I am afraid I am going to have trouble with that boy.

I haven't flirted, Mother. I can't help it if people like me. I've made up my mind. If Fred asks me to marry him, I will accept. I'm not madly in love, but I like him and we get along. He is handsome, young, and clever and very rich—even more than the Laurences.

One of us must marry well. Meg didn't. Jo won't. And Beth is too young. I wouldn't marry a man I hated, I promise. I know that in time I will grow to love Fred. I know he is fond of me. I can see it in the things he does.

One day he came hurrying to tell that he had a letter begging him to come home because Frank is very ill. He said when he left, 'I shall soon come back. Don't forget me.'

We will soon meet in Rome. If I don't change my mind, I'll say 'Yes, thank you' when he asks.

Don't worry about me. I won't do anything too quick. I wish I could see you for a good talk, Marmee.

Always, your Amy.

Tender Troubles

"I'm worried about Beth," Mrs. March said to Jo one day. "It's not her health, it's her spirits. I want you to find out what is on her mind."

When Jo asked why she thought this, her mother explained that Beth didn't talk to her father like she used to, sat alone, and was crying over Meg's babies. "Her songs are always sad ones. This isn't like Beth. I'm worried."

Jo reminded her mother that Beth was now eighteen and growing up.

"I'll take care of Beth's troubles and then tell you mine," Jo said.

Jo watched Beth and finally decided on what she believed might be wrong with her. While looking out the window one day, someone passed by and called out.

Beth leaned forward and smiled. "How strong and well and happy that dear boy looks."

Jo watched Beth and then slipped away. "Goodness, Beth loves Laurie! I never dreamed of such a thing." She stared at the boy's picture on the wall. "It would be awful if he doesn't love her back. He must. I'll make him!"

Jo watched Laurie that night closer than ever before. As usual, Beth lay on the sofa and Laurie sat in a low chair nearby, telling her all types of stories and gossip. Sometimes he bent low and talked quietly to her, seemed a little forgetful, and settled the afghan on Beth's feet in a gentle way.

Who knows? thought Jo. *Stranger things have happened.*

Jo felt that she should get out of the way and searched for a place to sit. She grabbed her favorite pillow. She took it to a corner and a few minutes later, Laurie sat down next to her and sighed.

Jo snapped at him, but he asked her to be nice. "After studying myself to a skeleton all week, a fellow deserves some nice treatment and should get it."

"Beth will treat you nice. I'm busy," Jo said.

Laurie said, "No, she's not to be bothered with me. But do you hate your boy?"

She told him that he should not be flirting all the time with silly girls. He promised that he had stopped and was ready for a modest girl.

Jo agreed, but told him that he should wait until he was done with college. "You're not half good enough for . . ." She stopped since she almost said her sister's name.

"No, I'm not," Laurie said, lowering his eyes.

That night, she heard a sob come from Beth. She ran to her bedside. "Is it your old pain?"

"No," Beth said. "A new one, but I can bear it."

"Tell me," Jo said.

Beth hugged her sister and cried. "You can't, there is no cure."

"I'll call Mother," Jo said. But Beth said she was better thanks to Jo's comfort.

Jo went to her mother a few days later and told her she wanted to go away somewhere that winter. "I want something new."

"Where?" her mother asked.

"To New York. Mrs. Kirke wrote to you about someone to teach her children and sew. I'll see new things to write about."

"Is that the only reason?" her mother asked.

Jo said, "I'm afraid Laurie is getting too fond of me. I love him as I always have, and that's all."

Her mother said, "Good. I don't think you are suited to one another except as friends."

The night before she left, Jo told Beth, "One thing I leave to your special care."

"You mean your writing papers?" Beth asked.

"No, my boy. Be very good to him."

Beth said, "I will, but he'll miss you and be sad. But I'll do my best." She wondered why Jo looked at her so strangely.

When Laurie said good-bye, he whispered, "It won't do a bit of good, Jo. My eye is on you. Be careful or I will come and bring you home."

Jo's journey to New York began in sadness as she lost sight of her father's face. But as she traveled, she began to enjoy it with all her heart. She was welcomed kindly from Mrs. Kirke. Even though the house was big and full of strangers in the school and boardinghouse, Jo liked the place very much.

On the way downstairs after seeing her room, she saw a man walk up behind a servant girl. The girl was carrying a heavy coal bucket, and he took it for her. When she asked about him, Mrs. Kirke explained that he was Professor Bhaer from Berlin, and he was always doing kind things.

The next day after the girls she was caring for went for a walk, Jo sat working on needlework. She heard someone humming a German tune. She peeked in a nearby room and saw Professor Bhaer. He was a large man with a bushy beard.

He was not handsome, but Jo immediately liked him.

Later, she decided to eat dinner with the other adults in the house rather than the children she watched over. She was shy about it, but curious. At the end of the table was the Professor.

The next evening Jo was sitting with Mrs. Kirke when Professor Bhaer came in to bring her newspapers. Jo and Professor Bhaer were

introduced. Later, she saw him trying to mend his socks and she felt sorry for him.

A few days after she heard a loud noise in the parlor. She entered and saw Professor Bhaer on his hands and knees with the children riding him like a horse. Jo stayed and enjoyed the fun and games of playing tag, dancing, and singing. She listened as the Professor told fairy stories to the children.

Soon, Jo and the Professor became very good friends. Jo agreed to do his mending to thank him for all the books he loaned her. He told her that he would teach her some German.

Jo wrote journals and letters to her mother. She was happy that Laurie seemed happy.

At Christmastime, Jo was wonderfully surprised by a box of gifts from home. And on New Year's Day, Professor Bhaer gave her a set of Shakespeare books. She had put little things around the room that he would find.

"I had a very happy New Year," she wrote home. *"I am cheerful all the time, work hard,*

and take more of an interest in other people than I used to."

Jo still found time for writing her stories. She took to writing the thrilling stories that were very popular. She took her first story to the editor of a newspaper. When she went back again, he said he would buy the story. But he did not like her trying to tell the moral of the story.

"People want to be entertained," he said.

He offered her twenty-five dollars and she agreed. Soon she was writing many stories full of bandits and gypsies. The readers did not care about correct grammar and punctuation or even if the stories were believable. Soon she had quite a bit of money saved. She wanted to take Beth to the mountains the next summer.

One thing bothered her about what she was doing. She could not tell her family back home of her stories. She had a feeling her parents would not approve.

One day, Professor Bhaer sat beside her. When he saw a newspaper with a picture of a crazy man, a dead man, a villain, and a snake, he talked of how much he disliked such stories.

Jo blushed. She was happy it wasn't the paper she wrote stories for, but she knew hers was like that story.

"People like these stories," she tried to say. "Many good people make a living writing them."

Professor Bhaer threw the paper into the fire. "Just because people like certain things that may harm them, it isn't right to give them such things."

Jo agreed with him and decided to burn her piles of newspapers with her stories in them. Now, three months of her work was a pile of ashes. Sometimes she wished Father and Mother hadn't raised her to be so careful about right and wrong. She decided to put her pen down for a while.

Jo stayed with Mrs. Kirke until June. Everyone seemed sorry to see her leave, especially the children. She told Professor

Bhaer that he should come see her sometime if he was ever traveling near her home. "Come next month when Laurie graduates."

"He is your best friend?" the Professor asked.

Jo said yes, and that she was very proud of him. She did not notice how Professor Bhaer's face changed when he thought that maybe Laurie was more than a friend to Jo.

"I'm afraid I cannot come, but I wish your friend the best and you all happiness."

Later, the Professor thought about Jo and leaned his head on his hands. Then, he walked around his room as if searching for something he could not find. "It is not for me. I must not hope for it," he said.

Early the next morning he went to the train station to say good-bye to Jo. Thanks to him, she began her journey home with a happy thought, *The winter is gone and I've written no books and not earned a fortune, but I've made a friend worth having. I will try to keep him all my life.*

Heartache

Laurie graduated from college with honors. The Marches and his grandfather were there to see him give a speech.

When Jo returned home, she met him for a walk but did not hold his arm as usual. Soon the talk between them was silent.

"You must take a good long vacation!" she said.

"I plan to," Laurie said.

Jo looked at him and saw him staring at her in a way that she knew the dreaded moment had come. She said, "No, Teddy, please don't!"

"I will," he said, grabbing her hand. "You must hear me. We've got to talk about it."

Jo promised to listen.

Laurie said, "I've loved you ever since I've known you, Jo. I can't wait any longer to tell you."

"I never wanted to make you care for me," Jo said. "I don't understand why I can't love you as you want. I've tried, but I can't change how I feel."

"Is this true, Jo?" Laurie asked.

Jo said, "Really, truly, dear."

Laurie dropped her hands and turned to go.

"I'm so sorry," Jo said. "People can't make themselves love someone. Laurie, I want to tell you something."

"No!" Laurie cried. "Don't tell me you love that old man." Laurie told her that he was talking about the professor she was always writing about from New York.

Jo laughed. "He isn't old or anything bad. He's the best friend I have next to you. I haven't the least idea of loving him or anyone else."

"I'll never love anyone else!" Laurie shouted.

Jo told him she still had not said what she

wanted to say. Having hope in his heart, he sat down on the grass at her feet.

"Everyone expects it of us. I can't go on without you. Say you will marry me and let's be happy!" Laurie said.

"I don't believe I will ever marry," Jo said. "I'm happy as I am."

Laurie jumped up and said, "You'll be sorry someday, Jo."

As he rowed away in his boat on the river, Jo went straight to Mr. Laurence and told him what happened. When Laurie came home, he played so sadly on the piano, his grandfather went to him and put kind hands on his shoulders.

"I know what has happened," Mr. Laurence said. He told Laurie that the best thing to do was to go away for a while. He had promised that Laurie could travel after college.

Laurie sighed and said sadly, "It doesn't matter where I go or what I do."

Beth's Secret

Jo could see the change in Beth when she came home that spring. Her heart was sad at the sight of Beth's thin face. Her skin looked almost as if you could see through it.

Jo showed Beth her savings for the mountain trip, but Beth begged not to go so far from home. She agreed to another small visit to the seashore. Jo and Beth went alone since Marmee did not want to leave her grandbabies.

One day when Jo thought Beth was asleep, she looked for color in Beth's checks but saw none. It came to her that Beth was slowly drifting away from her.

Beth looked up at her and said, "Jo, I'm glad you know. I've tried to tell you, but I couldn't. Don't be sad about me."

"Is this why you were so unhappy in the fall?" Jo asked.

"Yes," Beth said. "I gave up hoping then, though I tried to pretend it wasn't so. When I saw you all so strong and full of plans, it was hard to feel I could never be like you."

"Oh, Beth," Jo could only cry.

"I didn't want to frighten you when Marmee was so worried about Meg, and with Amy away and you happy with Laurie—I thought."

"I thought you loved him and I went away because I couldn't," cried Jo.

Beth was surprised. "But he could never be anything but a brother to me."

"You must get well!" Jo said.

"I want to," Beth said. "I try every day. But every day I get a little worse."

Beth made Jo promise to tell her family when they got home, but Jo hoped they would see it on their own.

Beth was quiet. "I don't know how to say this, but I believe I was never intended to live as long. I never had plans for when I grew up like you all or ever thought about being married. I'm not afraid, but I feel I will be homesick for you even in heaven."

Jo said, "Amy is coming home in the spring and you shall be ready to see her. I'm going to have you well by then."

But Beth said, "Don't hope any more. It won't do any good. We will enjoy being together while we can and have happy times."

Jo leaned down to kiss Beth's sweet face. She dedicated herself completely to Beth.

When they got home, Mother and Father saw what they had hoped was not true. Beth went straight to bed. Father leaned his head against the fireplace and did not turn. Mother held her arms out to Jo as if for help. Jo ran to comfort her without a word.

New Impressions

On Christmas Day in Nice, France, it was a beautiful day for a walk. A tall young man walked slowly. There were plenty of pretty girls to see, but he didn't pay attention except to look at some blonde girl or someone in a blue dress as if watching for someone.

Then a woman hurried down the streets. The young woman, a blonde, was dressed in blue. He waved his hat at her like a little boy.

"Laurie, is it really you? I thought you'd never get here!" Amy cried.

Laurie said, "I promised to spend Christmas with you and here I am."

They climbed into a carriage and drove away as Amy told him about the Christmas party at their hotel that evening.

He told her how he had spent a month in Berlin, then joined his grandfather in Paris. "He will be there with friends for the winter."

Laurie explained that his grandfather hated to travel and he hated to stay still. So while Mr. Laurence stayed with friends, Laurie could travel and then go back to see him. He praised Amy when she spoke French and told her how charming she was. Amy blushed, but she didn't like the new way he spoke. She wished he had stayed more like the boy he had been.

Amy went to the post office to get letters from home. She was sad at the word that Beth was doing poorly and thought about going home, but her mother had told her to stay.

That night she dressed up very nice. She saw her old friend Laurie in a new light, not as 'our boy,' but as a handsome man. She wore an old white silk ball dress. She put up her hair and put bunches of azalea flowers in her skirts.

When Laurie arrived, he complimented her and she complimented how nice he looked.

He gave her flowers in a little holder for her wrist. They danced together until others came to dance with her. When he sat down to watch as she danced, he studied her and decided that little Amy was going to make a very charming woman.

When she was done dancing, Laurie hurried away to bring her some food. He devoted himself to her for the rest of the evening. Their interest in one another grew, even without them knowing.

But soon Amy began to see things in Laurie she did not like. He promised to go visit his grandfather, but did not. She and her aunt began calling him 'Lazy Laurence,' but it did not bother him.

He told her also about how Jo did not love him the way he loved her. Then he got angry when Amy called him Teddy, the name Jo always called him. They argued back and forth until finally Amy gave him the sketch she had been working on.

He stared at the long, lazy figure on the grass, with half-shut eyes and a listless face.

"You draw so well!" he said. "It's me."

Amy laid another sketch beside it. "That is as you are, this is as you were."

The older sketch was full of life and spirit. It was of him taming a horse, and his attitude was full of energy and meaning. He blushed from the lesson she had given him.

They laughed and talked all the way home. When he bent to kiss her hand, she told him to be himself. He gave her a hearty English handshake as before.

The next morning he sent her a note. It said, *"Tell your aunt good-bye. Your 'Lazy Laurence' has gone to his grandfather. Have a wonderful winter."*

"I'm glad he's gone," Amy said. Her smile turned to a frown as she looked around the empty room. "I am glad, but I will miss him!"

The Valley of Shadows

When the first pain of knowing Beth's illness was over, the family accepted what would come and tried to help one another. They put away their grief and did what they could to make the last year a happy one.

Beth had the nicest room in the house. Everything she loved was put there—flowers, pictures, her piano, and her cats. Father's best books, Mother's chair, Jo's desk, and Amy's finest drawings were also there. Every day Meg brought her babies to bring joy to Auntie Beth. John set aside some money to give Beth the fruit she loved. Hannah made special foods to help Beth's appetite, crying as she worked.

Nothing changed Beth's sweet and unselfish personality. Even as she prepared to leave life, she tried to make it happier for the ones who would stay behind. She enjoyed making little things for schoolchildren passing by, sometimes dropping a pair of mittens out the window. The children thought of her as a fairy godmother, showering gifts on them.

The first few months were very happy with everyone sitting in her room. It was a peaceful time given to them before the sad hours to come.

Soon, Beth said that the needles she sewed with were too heavy and put them down forever. Talking tired her and faces upset her. She was filled with pain.

There came long nights and heavy days. Everyone's heart ached as they prayed. Those who loved her most were forced to see thin hands stretched out to them and cry out, "Help me, help me!"

As her body completely weakened, Beth's soul grew strong. Though she said little, everyone knew she was ready.

Jo never left her after Beth said, "I feel stronger when you are here." She slept on a couch in the room and woke up often to feed or wait on her sister, who rarely asked for anything.

Many times when she woke up, Jo would see Beth reading her *Pilgrim's Progress* book or hear her softly singing. Sometimes she had her face in her hands, tears dropping through the thin fingers.

One night Beth found a little piece of paper written by Jo. She decided to read it while Jo was asleep. It was a beautiful poem written about Beth. Jo wrote of all the things that Beth was in life—the sweet, kind, and patient person. Jo asked that Beth would leave these things to her and help Jo become a better person.

It meant so much to Beth to know that her simple life had not been useless. When Jo woke, Beth said, "I found this and read it. Have I been all this to you?"

Jo put her head next to Beth's. "Oh Beth, so much!"

"I'm not afraid of death anymore," Beth said. "You must take my place, Jo, and be everything to Mother and Father. Remember that love is the only thing that we can carry with us when we go. It makes the end so easy."

"I'll try," Jo said. She promised herself a new and better desire in life.

The spring days came and went. The flowers bloomed and the birds came back in time to say good-bye to Beth. She clung to the hands that led her all her life as Father and Mother guided her through the Valley of the Shadow and gave her up to God.

As Beth had hoped, the "tide went out easily." In the dark hour before the morning, she quietly drew her last breath.

Mother and her sisters cried as they saw the beautiful peace on Beth's face that replaced all the pain.

When morning came, the fire was out and Jo's place was empty. The room was still, but a bird sang on a nearby branch. Sunshine came in the window onto the peaceful face on the pillow. Her face was so full of painless peace that they all smiled through their tears and thanked God that Beth was finally well.

Laurie and Amy

The speech that Amy had given Laurie in Nice did him good. But, he would not admit it for a long time afterward.

Whenever he felt joy or sadness, he put it into a song. The next time his grandfather found Laurie getting tired of being quiet, he ordered him to go somewhere. Laurie went to Vienna to visit musical friends. But soon he found that the kind of music he tried was too hard. Instead, he thought of the dancing tunes from the Christmas ball in Nice.

For a while he tried to write operas. Finally, he tore up his sheets of music. He decided Amy was right and he could not be what he wasn't.

"Now what shall I do?"

He thought the job of forgetting his love for Jo would take up all his energy for years. But he was surprised to find it became easier every day. He tried to make himself feel the same love, but soon found that his boyish love was going away.

But he could not give up trying. He grabbed a pen and paper and wrote to Jo. He told her he could not do anything else until he knew there was no hope of her changing her mind. She wrote back that she couldn't love him that way and was too busy taking care of Beth. She begged him to be happy with someone else. She also asked him not to tell Amy that Beth was worse.

He decided to write Amy, who wrote back how homesick she was. Soon their letters were going back and forth. He went back to Paris, hoping Amy would ask him to come to Nice. But Amy was having her own life that she did not wish Laurie to see.

Fred Vaughn had returned and asked her to marry him. She changed her answer from yes to "No, thank you." She decided she needed more than money and fame. Laurie's face kept returning to her thoughts.

Amy told Laurie in her next letter that Fred had gone to Egypt. Laurie was glad to hear it, but he felt sorry for Fred. He knew what it was like to be turned down.

Sadly, the letter telling Amy that Beth was dying never reached her. When the next letter did arrive, Beth was already buried. Her family had said that she should not shorten her visit since it was too late to say good-bye to Beth. They hoped her absence would make her sadness easier. But she wanted to be home and every day waited for Laurie to come and comfort her.

The moment Laurie read his own letter from home about Beth, he packed up and went to Amy. He found her in an old garden, leaning her head on her hand. She was homesick and thinking of Beth. Laurie watched her a moment, seeing her with new eyes. When she saw him, she ran to him.

"Oh, Laurie, I knew you'd come to me!"

They knew then what was important. Amy felt no one could comfort her as well as Laurie. He decided Amy was the only woman in the world who could fill Jo's place and make him happy. They talked of their loss.

The moment her aunt saw Amy's face, she understood that Amy had been longing for Laurie all along. She invited Laurie to stay. Laurie was never lazy there. He walked, rode, boated, and studied, while Amy was happy with everything he did.

In spite of their sorrow, it was a very happy time. Laurie did not rush telling her he loved her. They both knew it and in the garden they decided they would become engaged.

Surprises

After Beth died, Jo found it hard to do anything she liked anymore. At night she would sometimes cry, "Oh Beth, come back!"

She soon found that comfort came through her parents. She begged her father to talk with her as he had to Beth. They had many good times together sitting in Beth's chair, talking about the things that upset Jo.

And later, talking with Meg, Jo discovered that Meg had grown in her life as a wife and mother. Jo wondered if marriage could help her to grow someday.

She enjoyed her talks with her mother, who encouraged her to write again. But Jo did not have the heart to write.

"If I did, nobody cares for my writings," she said.

"Write something for us and never mind the rest of the world," her mother said.

Jo pulled out her old stories and began working on them. An hour later, her mother looked in and saw Jo writing away. She left with a smile.

With love and sorrow in her life, Jo worked hard and sent her stories away. They were welcomed and soon were published.

When Amy and Laurie wrote about being engaged, Jo was a little sad at first. But she quickly talked about the hopes and plans she had for them. Jo was glad Amy learned to love him, but admitted she was lonely. Amy's happiness woke feelings in her own heart to have what her sisters did.

Jo later found some books from her time at Mrs. Kirke's. There was a message from the Professor in one that took on new meaning.

"Wait for me, my friend. I may be a little late, but I shall surely come."

If he only would! Jo thought. She missed him and put her head down to cry as the rain fell outside.

Jo lay on an old sofa thinking about her birthday the next day. She was almost twenty-five and felt she had nothing to show for it.

"I'm an old maid," she said. "I have a pen for a husband and stories as my children."

Jo must have fallen asleep, for she suddenly thought she saw Laurie's ghost standing in front of her. She stared at him in surprise when he bent down and kissed her.

"My Teddy!" she shouted.

"You are glad to see me, dear Jo?"

"I can't tell you how happy I am! Where is Amy?" Jo asked.

"We stopped at Meg's and your mother and sister won't let my wife go," Laurie said.

Jo cried, "Your what?"

Laurie said, "Oh dear, I've done it now."

Jo shouted, "You've gotten married? Tell me what happened."

"We planned to come home a month or more ago," he began. "Grandpa wanted to come home and I couldn't let him go alone, but I could not leave Amy either. So, I said, 'Let's get married.' We talked it over with your aunt and there wasn't time to write to ask about doing it then."

"When, where, and how?" Jo asked.

Laurie said, "Six weeks ago in Paris. It was a very quiet wedding. Even in our happiness we couldn't forget dear little Beth. We wanted to surprise you. But my grandfather wasn't ready to leave for a month and sent us off on our honeymoon trip."

He told her, "I shall never stop loving you, but the love has changed and I have learned to see it is better this way. Amy and you have changed places in my heart. I believe it was meant to be this way. Can we go back to the happy times when we first knew one another?"

"We will be brother and sister all our lives," Jo said.

Laurie said he was sorry she was there to bear all the sorrow of Beth's death. She said she had Mother and Father to help her, but she was lonely at times.

"You won't be lonely again," he said. "We need you to help us learn how to keep house and let us love you."

Then he stood with a happy look on his face as Amy's voice called, "Where is she? Where's my dear Jo?"

The whole family came in and hugged and kissed one another. Yet Jo felt lonely.

Suddenly, there came a knock at the porch door. Jo opened the door and stepped back as if a ghost had come to surprise her. A tall, bearded gentleman smiled at her.

"Oh, Professor Bhaer, I am so glad to see you!" she cried.

He told her he was happy to see her, but at the sound of voices and dancing feet, he said,

"Oh, you have a party—"

Jo invited him in. "It's only the family. My sister and others have come home."

He told her she looked as if she had been sick.

"Not ill, but tired and sad. We have had trouble since I saw you last," she said.

He shook her hand and said, "My heart was sore for you when I heard about your sister."

Jo introduced him to her parents. Her face and voice was full of pride and happiness. They all gave him a friendly welcome. Jo noticed how nice he looked and couldn't help being happy to see him. Laurie thought him the most wonderful old fellow he had ever met.

When Professor Bhaer said good-bye to Mrs. March, he promised to come again since he had business left to do. Jo wondered what his business might be. If she had seen his face when he looked at her picture, she might have understood, especially when he turned off the light and kissed the picture in the dark.

Chapter 20

Under the Umbrella

Jo often met Professor Bhaer on her long walks. Both pretended it was an accident that they happened to meet. She made sure that there was coffee for supper when he visited because the Professor didn't like tea.

By the second week, everyone knew what was going on and tried to pretend they didn't. They didn't ask why Jo sang when she worked or did her hair up three times a day.

Then suddenly the Professor stayed away for three whole days. Jo was very upset, thinking he had just gone home.

When she got ready to go for her usual walk, Mrs. March mentioned several things Jo could get her in town. "And," she added, "if you happen to see Professor Bhaer, invite him home to tea."

Jo kissed her mother and thought about how good Marmee was to her. As she walked, it began to rain.

"It serves me right!" Jo said. "Why did I put on all my best clothes and come down here, hoping to see the Professor?"

She hurried through the streets with rain all around her ankles. Then she noticed an umbrella over her head. She looked up to see Professor Bhaer.

"I'm shopping," she told him.

Professor Bhaer smiled. "May I go also and take for you the packages?"

"Yes, thank you," Jo said.

As they walked she said, "We thought you had gone."

"I wouldn't leave without saying good-bye to those who have been so kind to me," he said.

He asked if she missed him. "I'm always glad to see you, sir," she said.

He promised to come to see her family one more time before he left.

"You are going then?" she asked.

He nodded and explained he had finished his business and found a job teaching at a college that was not nearby. He helped her shop and she liked him more every moment they talked.

"Shall we go home?" he asked.

She said she was tired, but her voice was sad. Her head ached and her heart felt as cold as her feet. Professor Bhaer was going away. He only cared for her as a friend. She decided the sooner it was over the better.

She turned away, blinking hard to hide the tears. When he saw them he said, "Heart's dearest, why do you cry?"

"Because you are going away," she said.

"That is so good!" cried Professor Bhaer. "Jo, I have nothing but much love to give you. I wanted to be sure I was more than a friend. Am I? Can you make a little place in your heart for old Fritz?"

"Oh yes!" Jo said.

Because of the rain and the fact that both their hands were full of packages, he could not propose on his knees or offer Jo his hand. The only way he could express his happiness was to look at her and smile.

"Why didn't you tell me all this sooner?" she shyly asked.

"I wanted to tell you when we said good-bye in New York, but I thought your friend was the one you loved, so I did not speak."

Jo said, "Teddy was only a boy and soon got over his love for me."

"Good," the Professor said. "I have waited so long and am selfish with my love for you."

He showed her a piece of worn paper from his pocket. She saw that it was one of the poems she had written and had published in a newspaper. It was about Jo and each of her sisters.

He said that the verse about her, where she mentioned being sad and lonely, showed him she would find comfort in true love. He explained that he had to keep his promise to go and teach. He asked if she could wait for him. She said that she could, knowing they loved one another.

They came to her house and she led him inside to the warmth of her family.

"Welcome home," Jo said.

CHAPTER 21

Harvest Time

For a year Jo and her Professor worked and waited. They met together at times and wrote long letters. The second year they still did not have much money.

Then Aunt March died suddenly. The family loved her in spite of her sharp tongue. But all were surprised to find she left her large home and land to Jo.

"You can sell it for a good deal of money," Laurie said.

Jo shook her head. "I won't."

Everyone was surprised. It was such a large house to take care of, especially with the garden and orchard. But Jo explained that she wanted to open a school for boys.

"It will be a happy homelike school with me to take care of them and Fritz to teach them," she said.

Her parents liked the idea. Mr. Laurence agreed. "It's a wonderful idea," he said. "Tell us about it."

Jo told them that she had always wanted to take care of poor, lonely boys with no mothers. When she had told Fritz about it, he said it was just what he would like to do.

"It's the perfect place for boys. The house is big and the furniture is strong. They could help in the garden and orchard," Jo said.

"But how will you pay for everything?" Laurie asked. "If the boys have no family you will not make any money."

Jo said, "Don't be silly. I will have some rich boys come first, then I can take in some poor boys. Rich people's children sometimes need special care, too."

That year things happened quickly. Before she knew it, Jo was married and they moved into Plumfield, her aunt's home. Then came six or seven boys, some poor as well as rich.

It was hard work, but Jo was happy. As the years went by, she had three boys of her own. It was a house full of boys.

Each of the March girls were happy with their own lives.

At the harvest celebration, Mrs. March told Jo, "I think your harvest will be a good one."

"Not as good as yours," Jo said. "We can never thank you enough for your patient sowing and reaping of us."

Mrs. March held out her arms and gathered her children and grandchildren to her.

"My girls, however long you live, I can never wish you greater happiness than this."